Nobody loves Fergie

NOVALIS

TWENTY-THIRD PUBLICATIONS
A Division of Bayard   MYSTIC, CT 06355

© 2002 Novalis, Saint Paul University, Ottawa, Canada

Cover design and layout: Caroline Gagnon

The illustrations were done using mixed technique: crayons, gouache and ink.

Business Office:
Novalis
49 Front Street East, 2nd Floor
Toronto, Ontario, Canada
M5E 1B3

Phone: 1-800-387-7164 or (416) 363-3303
Fax: 1-800-204-4140 or (416) 363-9409
E-mail: cservice@novalis.ca

Published in the United States by
Twenty-Third Publications
A Division of Bayard
185 Willow Street
P.O. Box 180
Mystic, CT 06355
(860) 536-2611
(800) 321-0411
www.twentythirdpublications.com

National Library of Canada Cataloguing in Publication Data

Cocks, Nancy, 1954–
    Nobody loves Fergie

(The new adventures of Fergie the frog)
ISBN 2-89507-274-4

Marton, Jirina II. Title. III. Series: Cocks, Nancy, 1954– .
New adventures of Fergie the frog.

PS8555.O2854N62 2002   jC813’.54   C2002-900888-3
PZ7

U.S. ISBN: 1-58595-224-9

Printed in Canada.

We acknowledge the financial support of the Government of Canada through the Book Publishing Industry Development Program (BPIDP) for our publishing activities.

10 9 8 7 6 5 4 3 2 1   10 09 08 07 06 05 04 03 02

In memory of my father, Jack,
who loved stories
—N.C.

To Leonard
—J.M.

One Saturday morning, Fergie the Frog hopped out of his mudhole to find his mother baking an algae food cake.

"Mmmm! I love algae food cake, Mom. But it's not my birthday. Why are you baking a cake?" Fergie asked.

"It's for Freddie. Your brother won his diving competition yesterday, so I thought we would have a little party for him at supper."

Fergie frowned. "If the cake is for Freddie, are you going to bake something else for me?"

"No, Fergie. Not today," said his mother. "Today is Freddie's special day."

Fergie was disappointed. "Where is Freddie, anyway?"

"I sent him to the store for some cream of caterpillar soup."

"Aw, Mom. Why couldn't I go to the store for you? I love going to the store. How come you always let Freddie go?"

"Fergie," his mother said, "I do not always let Freddie go to the store for me. He was up first this morning so I sent him. If you want to give me a hand, you could pick up the garbage around the swamp. Then the house will be clean for the party."

Fergie hopped away in a huff. "Hmmph. Freddie always gets things *his* way. *He* wins diving competitions. *He* gets a party. *He* gets a cake. *He* gets to go to the store. And I have to pick up the garbage. Nobody around here likes me. Everybody likes Freddie best," Fergie thought.

As Fergie did his work, he felt sadder and madder. "I'm not going to this dumb party. I'm going to stay in my mudhole. Freddie can have his stupid party by himself."

When the swamp shore was clean, Fergie threw himself into the mud.

Later in the afternoon, the guests began to arrive: Fergie's grandma, Uncle Skip and Aunt Glossy, and Freddie's diving pal, Webster. Fergie could smell the bug burgers on the barbecue. He felt even sadder. A tear rolled down his nose.

"Nobody likes me," he sighed. "Everybody likes Freddie best."

Someone called out, "Let's have a toast to the greatest little diver in the swamp. Raise your swamp water soda to Freddie!"

"To Freddie!" everyone cried.

Freddie blushed bright green. "Thanks for the party and the cake," he said. "But I'm not the greatest diver in the swamp yet. I just had a couple of lucky leaps yesterday. And I want to thank Fergie for coming to practice with me all summer. He watched to see if I held my toes just right. Thanks, Fergie," said Freddie, looking around. "Hey, where is Fergie?"

No one had noticed that Fergie wasn't there.

"I think Fergie is feeling a little blue," said Mother Frog. "Maybe you should take him a piece of cake and thank him nose to nose," she added.

Freddie hopped over to the mudhole with a piece of cake. "Fergie, I'm sorry you're feeling bad," he said. "I hope you'll have a piece of my cake. Thanks for helping me at diving practice."

Another tear rolled down Fergie's nose. It's hard to be mad at someone who gives you a piece of cake, he thought to himself. "I'm glad you won, Freddie," Fergie gulped. "Maybe you could help me with my dives for next year, so that I can have a party too?"

"Sure," said Freddie. "Let's start tomorrow if you're feeling better."

"I'm already feeling better," said Fergie as he ate his piece of cake.

When somebody else wins prizes and gets a special party, we may feel left out. When our brother or sister gets a cheer, we might think nobody likes us that much. But God always loves each of us in a special way. God's love is deeper than the ocean. God's love flows like a river. There is enough for everyone to share.

God, when I feel lonely or left out, come and be with me. Fill me with your love so that I know I am special in your eyes.